For Master Rafe Peacock - J.W.

For Mel - G.P.

PUFFIN BOOKS Published by the Penguin Group:

London, New York, Australia, Canada, India, Ireland, New Zealand and South Africa

Penguin Books Ltd, Registered Offices: 80 Strand, London WC2R ORL, England

puffinbooks.com   First published 2008 Published in this edition 2012 007 - 10 9 8 7

Manufactured in China ISBN: 978-0-141-50003-4

There's an Ouch in my Pouch!

Written by Jeanne Willis

Illustrated by Garry Parsons

PUFFIN

What is the matter
with Willaby Wallaby?
Why is he sobbing
and throwing a wobbly?

Willaby Wallaby's not where he wants to be.

Where does he want to be?

Inside the
pouch!

Once it was perfect and fitted him properly . . .

Now it is terribly, horribly knobbly.

Now it is wodgy and wedgy and wriggly.

No wonder Willaby Wallaby's niggly.

Ma says to Willaby,
"Don't be so sillaby.
Willaby, will you get
back in your pouch?

Let's have a talk about
why you went walkabout."

Willaby shouts,
"It's because of the OUCH!"

Off bounces Willaby, bibbly-bobbly boingy-boing boing to the BLUE BILLABONG.

There's Mummy Wombat,
all tummy and sun hat.

She says to him,
"Willaby, tell me what's wrong!"

Willaby shouts,
"There's an Ouch
in my Pouch!

It is making me grumpy.
It's making me grouch.

Atishoo! Atishoo!

I'm catching a chillaby.
Please give a pouch to a
poor little wallaby."

"Come along, chummy!
I'll be your new mummy,
no worries!" says Wombat.
"You hop right inside."

But her pouch is
ROOMY,
too woolly and gloomy,
too baggy, too saggy,
too bulgey and
too

WIDE.

Off bounces Willaby,

bibbly-bobbly

boingy-boing

boing

to the BLUE BILLABONG.

There's Mummy Possum
curled up in the blossom.
She says to him,
"Willaby, tell me what's wrong."

Willaby shouts,
"There's an Ouch in my Pouch!
It is making me grumpy.
It's making me grouch.

Atishoo!

Atishoo!

I'm catching a chillaby.
Please give a pouch to a poor little wallaby."

"My pouch is ripper for
housing a nipper," says Possum.
"Climb in and I'll soon
have you chipper."

But her pouch is too

LOUD.

It is **noisy** Down Under.

Her tummy is **rumbling**

louder than thunder.

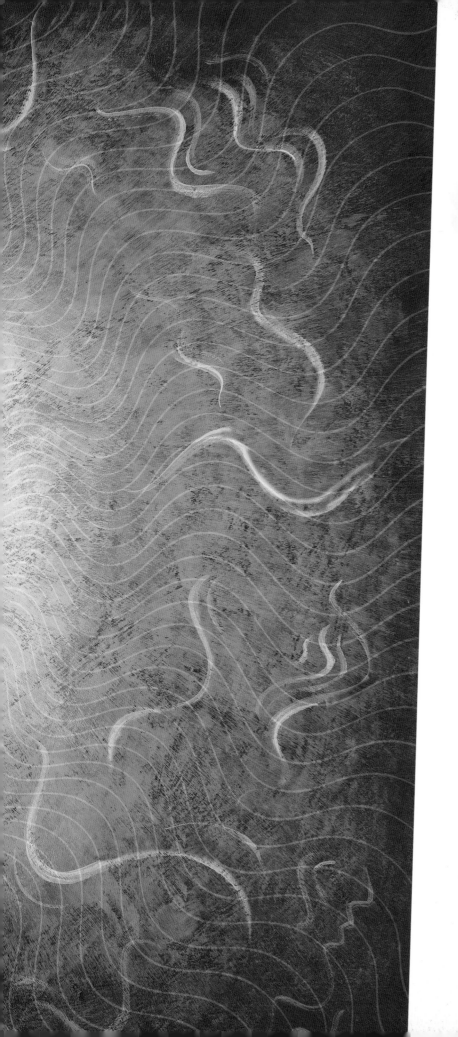

Off bounces Willaby,

bibbly-bobbly

boingy-boing

boing

to the **BLUE BILLABONG.**

There's Mummy Dingo
just doing her thing-o.
"*Hey, little drongo,*"
she drools,
  "*what is wrong?*"

Willaby shouts,
  "There's an
  Ouch in my Pouch!
It is making me grumpy.
    It's making me grouch.

Atishoo!

Atishoo!

I'm catching a chillaby.
Please give a pouch to
a poor little wallaby."

Now, wombats and possums and tree kangaroos
and koalas have pouches, but here's the bad news –
Ma Dingo's a dog and A DOG HAS NO POUCH,
but she swears that her pouch is as soft as a couch.

"*Come closer!*" she growls.
"It is not on my belly.
Come closer. You'll love it.
There's even a telly . . .

. . . it's inside my mouth
on the tip of my tongue!"

Run for your life, little Willaby, run!

Off bounces Willaby,

bibbly-bobbly boingy-boing boing

he goes back to his mum.

Willaby Wallaby blubbers. Boo hoo!
Ma gives him a cuddle.
"You poor little roo,
but why did you ever
jump out of the pouch?"

"I was kicked out!" he says,
"by a terrible OUCH!"

"That's not an **Ouch**, silly!"
Ma says to Willaby.
"That's **BABY JILLABY!**"

Oh, what a thrillaby!
"Move over, Jillaby!
Share with your brother,
there's room in my pouch for you both,"
says their mother.

Willaby almost jumps in –
then he stops.

He liked being
free to do

bounces

and

hops. . .

"I don't need a pouch," he says.
"Give it to Sis.
It's for wallaby babies!
I've grown out of this.
I am a BIG boy,
I'm brave and I'm strong!"

And off they all bounce to the BLUE BILLABONG.

THE END